BANDSLAM:
THE MOVIE SCRAPBOOK

Adapted by Nicole Corse

Based on the screenplay by Josh A. Cagan and Todd Graff

PSS!
PRICE STERN SLOAN

Copyright © 2009 Summit Entertainment, LLC and Walden Media, LLC. All Rights Reserved.
Artwork © 2009 Summit Entertainment, LLC and Walden Media, LLC. All rights reserved.
Published by Price Stern Sloan, a division of Penguin Young Readers Group,
345 Hudson Street, New York, New York 10014.
PSS! is a registered trademark of Penguin Group (USA) Inc.

ISBN 978-0-8431-3486-5   10 9 8 7 6 5 4 3 2 1

SUMMIT ENTERTAINMENT AND WALDEN MEDIA PRESENT A GOLDSMITH-THOMAS PRODUCTION "BANDSLAM" ALY MICHALKA VANESSA HUDGENS GAELAN CONNELL SCOTT PORTER AND LISA KUDROW MUSIC SUPERVISORS LINDSAY FELLOWS LINDA COHEN EDITOR JOHN GILBERT, A.C.E. PRODUCTION DESIGNER JEFF KNIPP DIRECTOR OF PHOTOGRAPHY ERIC STEELBERG EXECUTIVE PRODUCERS RON SCHMIDT MARISA YERES PRODUCED BY ELAINE GOLDSMITH-THOMAS STORY BY JOSH A. CAGAN SCREENPLAY BY JOSH A. CAGAN AND TODD GRAFF DIRECTED BY TODD GRAFF

PG PARENTAL GUIDANCE SUGGESTED
SOME MATERIAL MAY NOT BE SUITABLE FOR CHILDREN
SOME THEMATIC ELEMENTS AND MILD LANGUAGE

  READ THE BOOKS FROM PENGUIN GROUP (USA) INC. SOUNDTRACK AVAILABLE ON HOLLYWOOD RECORDS

WALDEN MEDIA   SUMMIT

© COPYRIGHT SUMMIT ENTERTAINMENT, LLC AND WALDEN MEDIA, LLC. ALL RIGHTS RESERVED.

www.BandslamMovie.com

WILL

Dear Rock Legend David Bowie,

I know it's been a while since I've written, but I just started a new school and I've actually been kinda busy. I know. I know. To be busy you need friends. The thing is, I actually have some at this school. I'm even managing a band. It all started when I met Charlotte Barnes, or Charlotte met me, whatever. One minute she's asking me to help her with this after-school art class thing for little kids and the next I'm the manager of her band. They were good, but now that we've found a real sound, it's great. The guys are really talented and Charlotte is like the coolest girl to ever exist. They're all seniors. I'm actually hanging out with cool seniors. It seems a little weird to me, too, but that's the way it is now.

We're going to perform in this competition called BandSlam. It's pretty big around here. And if we win, we get an actual record deal! Do you want to come? We're competing against the school favorites, The Glory Dogs. They're not bad. They've got this super New Jersey, Bruce Springsteen, All-American thing going on. I really hope we beat them.

I guess I should tell you about Sa5m, too. Sa5m is, well, Sa5m. The five is silent. She's totally different from anyone else I've ever met. She's funny and sarcastic and kind of a loner, but I think she's perfect. Oh, wait, that's Sa5m at the door now. Well, that's all the time I have, gotta go!

Your #1 fan,
Will Burton

MEET WILL

I think I just kind of missed the memo about how to fit in in Cincinnati.

"SCHOOL ISN'T GUT-WRENCHINGLY AWFUL. MOSTLY IT'S JUST KINDA LIKE NOVOCAIN FOR THE SOUL."

It's a brand new year at Will's high school in Cincinnati, Ohio. He really doesn't want to go back. He's an outcast and everyone picks on him—constantly. But maybe things will change for the better. They can't get any worse, right?

CLIQUE BREAKDOWN

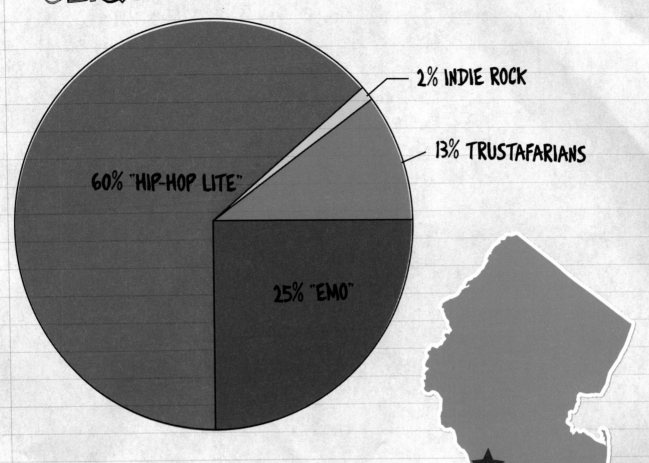

2% INDIE ROCK

13% TRUSTAFARIANS

60% "HIP-HOP LITE"

25% "EMO"

NEW JERSEY

KAREN

Will really needs a change. Luckily Will's mom Karen is offered a job in Lodi, New Jersey—just in time!

Good-bye Ohio! Hello New Jersey! New life, new school, new start. Things will definitely be different this time.

WELCOME TO MARTIN VAN BUREN HIGH SCHOOL

Unfortunately, high school in New Jersey seems exactly like high school in Ohio. It's got the same annoying bullies, boring teachers, and cliché cliques. At first the only upside is that no one knows who Will is.

But wait—there is something different about Van Buren. During lunch a ridiculously perfect-looking upperclassman takes the stage and says:

"Hey there, Van Buren! What's going to happen 3,600 hours from now?"

"BANDSLAM!"

"And who's going to take home the gold?"

"THE GLORY DOGS!"

"ALL THOSE YEARS OF WISHING I COULD MAKE MYSELF INVISIBLE—TURNS OUT ALL I HAD TO DO WAS MOVE TO NEW JERSEY."

BandSlam? The Glory Dogs? Will has no clue what's going on, but he's curious. So he asks the only other person sitting at his lunch table—a girl who seems a little out of place, too. She doesn't dress like anyone else, and she doesn't even look up from her book when she answers Will's questions. But at least she answers. Her name is Sa5m. (The 5 is silent.)

Will: "Exactly how big a deal is this BandSlam thing around here?"

Sa5m: "Texas-high-school-football big. You're new."

After exchanging class schedules, they discover they are in the same human studies class. Maybe this year will be different after all . . .

THE CHARACTERS

"I'm so busy doing things I would never do, I forget how freaked out I should be."

Will Burton knows more about music than any normal high school student. He's always been a little bit of an outsider, but once he becomes the manager of Charlotte's band, he fits right in. Will used to write a lot of letters to his idol, David Bowie, but now that he has a band to lead, he barely even has time to talk to his mom.

"Always do the thing that scares you."

Charlotte Barnes befriends Will and helps him drop his outcast status. She used to be the lead singer of Ben Wheatly and the Glory Dogs and now she's starting her own band. Charlotte was once head cheerleader and the most popular girl in school. No one really knows what made this ex-suburban princess prom queen change her ways . . . but it's sure to come out eventually.

Sa5m, a true original, is always hiding behind a book. Aside from reading, her favorite thing to do is use a Twizzler as a straw. She is usually alone, and pretends to like things that way. But her friendship with Will may make this shy beauty come out of her shell.

"The 5 is silent."

Karen will do anything for her son, Will. This includes keeping up on the latest video games so she can play with Will. She trains companion animals for the elderly, but she gets joy from hanging out with Will.

"You touch my kid, you die."

Meet Ben Wheatly
and the Glory Dogs

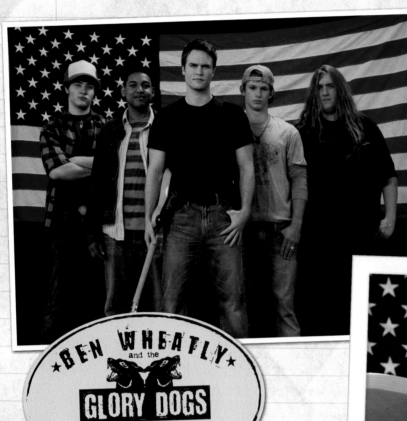

Last year, Ben Wheatly and the Glory Dogs performed at BandSlam and tied for second place with a band called the Burning Hotels. This year, they have their sights set on first place and don't mind stepping on a few paws in the process.

★BEN WHEATLY★
and the
GLORY DOGS
★ ★ ★ ★
RULING VAN BUREN SINCE 2006

Ben Wheatly
Lead singer

"THEY'RE GREAT, IN THAT NEW JERSEY, CHEVY IMPALA, SPRINGSTEEN KIND OF WAY."

Ben Wheatly, the leader of the band, is a natural star. He's just not that original of a star, since he closely modeled his look after an already established rocker (see Bruce Springsteen).

"THIS YEAR THERE'RE SOME NEW DOGS IN THE POUND."

Quinton Pearce

Instrument: Bass

His nickname is "Downtown" Quinton Pearce—no one is sure why. He plays a mean bass.

Bo Betreaux

Instrument: Drums

Bo likes drums, drums like Bo. Enough said.

Dylan Dyer

Instrument: Guitar

Dylan transferred schools just to play with Ben Wheatly and the Glory Dogs. He lives with his dad, and they don't get along, but hey, anything for the music, right?

Ben Wheatly and the Glory Dogs' Groupies

These ladies sell T-shirts, scream their heads off at concerts, and dream about dating a Glory Dog. Keep dreaming, ladies.

BUDDY UP

Will is relieved to get to his human studies class. At least he knows one person there, Sa5m, even if she isn't very talkative. Then their teacher makes the announcement that Will always dreads—"buddy up." They will be doing a project where each pair has to get to know each other and present their findings to the class in a creative way.

Everyone frantically pairs off and soon Will and Sa5m are the only ones left without a partner. They're stuck with each other. In an effort to break the ice, Will asks, "So I guess we're supposed to get to know each other. What's your favorite color?" After a second, Will realizes Sa5m is wearing all black, even down to her nail polish. Okay, so maybe that wasn't the ideal first question, but he had to start somewhere.

"BY SUMMER WE'RE GOING TO KNOW EACH OTHER IN WAYS WE NEVER EXPECTED."

Will: "What's your favorite color?"

Sa5m: "Guess."

Will: "Pink."

So Sa5m isn't the most approachable girl at Van Buren. It's only a small project, it doesn't really matter if he gets to know her or not, right?

Scratch that. This project is worth half of their grade! Sa5m and Will are going to have to be friends.

Will: "Maybe we should, I don't know, hang out after school somewhere and let stuff bubble up naturally."

Sa5m: "Like vomit?"

Will can already tell that this project is not going to be easy. He and Sa5m decide to meet at the mall after school to get started. But, once they get there, they don't seem to be making any progress. They definitely haven't "distilled each other down to their essence" as their teacher advised. Then Will suggests, "Why don't we take each other to our most favorite spot and our least favorite spot in the whole world?" They both agree that the mall is their mutual least favorite spot. Good. They can check that off the list.

DAY CARE

The next day at school, Will is almost run over by a stampede of huge jocks. They're like a herd of wild animals. Will gets out of the way just in time, but a girl isn't so lucky. Ben Wheatly practically runs her over and she drops her cello case. Ben is less than apologetic. Will rushes over to help her out, but the girl, Irene Lerman, isn't interested. No one touches her cello except for her.

"ARE YOU ALL RIGHT?"

The effortlessly cool Charlotte Barnes witnesses Will's attempt at kindness. She figures that the after-school day care program she leads could really use a nice guy like him.

Charlotte leads Will to the after-school program room. It's complete chaos with at least a dozen first-graders attempting to make art. She tosses them some beef jerky, which seems to quiet them down, at least for now, and introduces them to Will.

Charlotte: "Hey. Good Samaritan. Do you like kids?"

Will: "What?"

Charlotte: "It's a simple question. Do you like kids? Of course you do. All Good Samaritans like kids. It's in the handbook. Come on, we don't have a lot of time."

"Okay, monsters, listen up. I'd like to introduce you to my new 'art'-ner in crime . . . Name?"

"Will. Will Burton."

"Charlotte Barnes. Ladies and gentlemen, Will Burton is in da house!!"

Will's never been introduced quite like that before. But before he can get his bearings, Charlotte swipes his MP3 player and decides to use it as background music for this session. After all, musical taste is the best gauge of a person's true identity. She hooks it up to the speakers, presses play, and out comes . . . classical music! Will couldn't be more embarrassed. As he tries to recover his MP3 player (and his dignity), Charlotte notices the kids are actually enjoying the music.

Charlotte: "Way to soothe the savage beast. You are a weirdo, aren't you, Will Burton. Okay, so I'll see you next Tuesday at three."

Will: "You want me to do this every week?!"

Charlotte: "You catch on."

15

THE GLORY DOGS
(not to be confused with Ben Wheatly and the Glory Dogs)

After a couple of days of after-school day care volunteering, Charlotte offers Will a ride home. It turns out Will lives close to Charlotte's favorite place, the Overlook. Detour! The Overlook is stunning. It has the best view in the city, so it's no wonder Charlotte loves it.

Charlotte decides to teach Will a thing or two about good music, since it just won't do for him to listen to classical music all of the time. But she hadn't counted on Will's musical knowledge putting hers to shame. Charlotte is impressed. She's never met anyone who knew more about good music than she did, which gives her a brilliant idea. She is starting a band and they could use input from someone like Will.

Will thinks it's weird that a cool senior like Charlotte would give him the time of day, so he asks Sa5m what she thinks.

"COME HEAR MY FRIENDS JAM ON SATURDAY. GIVE US THE BENEFIT OF YOUR VAST MUSICAL KNOWLEDGE."

Will: "What's with Battle of the Bands around here? It's like a town obsession."

Charlotte: "That's because the winner gets a genuine, bona fide record deal."

Will: "Do you know Charlotte Barnes?"

Sa5m: "Be careful, Will. Leopards and cheerleaders don't change their spots."

The Band

Charlotte Barnes

Instrument: Rhythm guitar and lead vocals

Trademark: Closing her eyes and "feeling" the lyrics

"You have to go for it, kiddo. Carpe diem."

Omar

Instrument: Guitar

Trademark: Speaking in a faux English accent (he's actually from Jersey) and sporting an attempt at a mustache.

"Brilliant!"

Bug

Instrument: Bass

Trademark: (see Flea from Red Hot Chili Peppers)

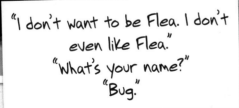

"I don't want to be Flea. I don't even like Flea."
"What's your name?"
"Bug."

Bun. E Carlos's software program

Instrument: Drums

Trademark: Not sounding like real drums

Charlotte's band isn't half bad, but they are definitely missing something—like a unique sound. They're going to need a lot of practice and work if they are going to stand a chance at winning BandSlam.

"We're the Glory Dogs. They're Ben Wheatly and the Glory Dogs; like Bruce Springsteen and the E Street Band. Or Tom Petty and the Heartbreakers. Get it? That way he can fire whoever he wants, whenever he wants to, and it stays his band."

Turns out everyone in the Glory Dogs is an ex-member of Ben Wheatly and the Glory Dogs. In fact, Bug claims he even came up with the band's name. Last year, they performed at BandSlam, but Ben dropped them after they lost. He didn't drop the drummer though, which explains why they are using beats from a computer.

"Ben didn't dump our old drummer, he just dumped us."

Will listens to the Glory Dogs perform. It's not that they aren't talented, it's just that they all seem to be playing solos. They aren't listening to each other. Their instruments aren't even tuned to one another's! They just don't sound like a group.

But they can fix it. So when Charlotte asks Will's opinion, he hesitantly gives it:

1. Bug, stop trying to be Flea from Red Hot Chili Peppers

2. Get a drummer

3. Listen to each other

4. Change the band's name

The rest of the band is a little annoyed with the new kid, but Charlotte runs with Will's suggestions. They only have a couple of months to prepare for BandSlam. Hopefully Will's superior musical knowledge will be enough to get them there. In the meantime, the band is starving—time for some local fine dining!

19

Hanging out at Jim's

Charlotte waits tables a few evenings a week at Jim's. The Glory Dogs and Ben Wheatly and the Glory Dogs both like to hang out there. This can cause some serious problems. Ben and Charlotte used to date, but she dumped him, and he's never quit trying to get her back.

Midway through dinner, Ben shows up. He comes over and gives his former bandmates a hard time until Charlotte asks him to leave. She still hasn't forgiven him for ditching Bug and Omar.

"I did not screw them over, Charlotte. I have a chance to play with real musicians. Dylan Dyer is an artist. You've said so yourself, right, Omar?"

But Ben isn't giving up without a fight. He just wants another shot with Charlotte. Too bad Charlotte wants nothing to do with him. When he asks her to hang out yet again, she says no, she's busy. Busy doing what?

Charlotte: "I'm hanging out with Will."

Ben: "Who the heck is Will?"

Charlotte: "That the heck is Will. Say hello, the heck is Will."

Will: "Hi."

"Will happens to be my friend. And the manager of our band. This year Van Buren is sending two bands to BandSlam."

What? The band is going to BandSlam? And, since when did Will become the band's manager? Actually, it kind of has a nice ring to it . . . Band Manager. Yeah, not bad at all.

THE QUEST FOR A FULLER SOUND

Now that Will is officially the manager of the band, his first task is to find a real drummer. All of the decent drummers are already in bands—except for one. Basher Martin. He even goes to their school, but they haven't talked to him yet because, well, he has been busy doing anger management. It's Will's job to get Basher on board. Will's definitely nervous about approaching him, but maybe Basher's anger management worked. Still, his name is Basher. Gulp.

Will heads to the school's shop class to find Basher. But he doesn't exactly like what he finds. Basher is completely scary! He's drumming away on the hood of a car and he does not seem to be in a good mood. Will wants to run for his life, but he has a band to lead now, so he walks right up and talks to Basher instead. Basher isn't very into the idea of being in a band, and even Will's flattery doesn't change his mind. But, when a picture of Will's mom pops up on Will's cell phone, Basher is suddenly very interested! He has a thing for older girls. And when Will promises that "the older babe" hangs out at the band's practices a lot, Basher joins the band.

"Keith Moon's dead, so he can't defend himself—but Moon used asparagus for sticks compared to me."

Basher: "Who's the babe?"
Will: "That's my . . . older sister."

Basher is exactly what the band needed. He rocks! They finally sound like a real band! But Will wants to make sure their sound fills the huge hall at BandSlam. He thinks a few sidemen will add the finishing touches to their sound. And he knows just who to ask . . .

Sideman: (noun) A musician who plays with a band when they need a fuller sound.

Irene Lerman
Instrument: Cello
Trademark: The toughest cello player you'll ever meet.

Kim Lee
Instrument: Piano
Trademark: Her concentration will not be broken, even if you switch her sheet music.

Marching band members
Instruments: Trumpet, trombone, saxophone
Trademark: They can't play without doing their marching band choreography.

23

JUGGLING HOME AND EVERYTHING ELSE

With the sidemen in place, the band finally finds its groove. Their sound is unique and quirky and totally fresh. Charlotte's almost on fire when she sings. Bug and Omar look like real rockers, and Basher has finally learned not to bash the drums to pieces every time he plays. Okay, so Irene and Kim aren't exactly rock and roll—but they sound great. And, yeah, it's a little awkward when the marching band members do their choreography, but it only adds to their charm! Plus, Charlotte showed Will a song that she wrote in her journal called "Someone to Fall Back On." Originally it was inspired by her dad, but the song really fits the band and will totally rock at BandSlam. The only thing left to work on before BandSlam is the band's name. Luckily, Will has already thought of the most perfect name ever . . .

Bug: "What do you want to call us?"

Will: "I Can't Go On, I'll Go On."

Basher: "I what I what I'll do what?"

24

i can't *t.*i*go

i can't go on* *i'll go on

At first, the band doesn't get the name. It is a little weird. But Charlotte likes it and convinces everyone that Will is always right when it comes to band stuff. They wouldn't be where they are without him—and where they are is SO much better than where they were.

Charlotte: "It's perfect. It's us. And more important, it's anyone who might like us."

How about: I Can't Have Sodium, I'll Have Sodium

I Can't Wear Horizontal Stripes, I'll Wear Horizontal Stripes

I Can't Drive Stick, I'll Drive Stick

I Can't Wear Blush, I'll Wear Blush

I Can't Do My Homework, I'll Do My Homework

I Can't Kiss You, I'll Kiss You

I Can't Walk the Dog, I'll Walk the Dog

I Can't Stay Awake, I'll Stay Awake

I Can't Whistle, I'll Whistle

I Can't Explain It, I'll Explain It

I Can't Sing Karaoke, I'll Sing Karaoke

I Can't Write in Cursive, I'll Write in Cursive

Write your own!

I Can't _____,

I'll _____

I Can't _____,

I'll _____

CBGB

Meanwhile, Will and Sa5m's group project deadline is approaching fast. And they still haven't even taken each other to their favorite places. They decide to go to Will's favorite place first. It's the world famous club, CBGB, in New York City.

Will and Sa5m have more fun than they ever expected to in NYC. They take pictures of just about everything on their cell phones, and Sa5m even plays a game of chess in Washington Square Park. They are really becoming friends. It's a new experience for both of them.

Sa5m: "We still have the stupid Human Studies project to finish and we haven't hung out since you've become Joe Cool Rock and Roll. You still haven't taken me to your favorite place."

Sa5m: "Come on."

Will: "You sure? There's going to be more than dust mites down there."

Sa5m: "Do the thing that scares you."

After exploring the city, Sa5m and Will finally make it to CBGB. It has been closed and empty for quite a while, so they can't go in. Or can they? Sa5m spots a broken lock on the hatch that leads down to the basement. They sneak down the concrete stairs and make their way into the main room. There isn't a bare spot on the graffiti-covered walls. Clearly this place is full of music history. Will climbs onto the stage and tries to take it all in. It's everything he imagined it would be, even if it is a little bit of a mess.

Will: "CBGB. The nerve center of everything that mattered in music for the past forty years. And it closed before I ever got to step inside. Now they're turning it into some cheesy clothes store."

Sa5m: "It's probably better. Now it will never disappoint you."

HISTORY OF CBGB

Opened in 1973, CBGB was originally meant to be a bluegrass club (Country, Bluegrass, and Blues). It was definitely not glamorous, but hey, rock 'n' roll never was, and besides, the rent was cheap. While almost no other places would let a band play without a record deal, CBGB's only rule was that a band be original and innovative, and new bands flocked to it. Punk music was born at CBGB, and, over the years, some of the coolest bands ever, played there, like the Ramones, Patti Smith, and Bad Brains. CBGB closed in October 2006 due to an increase in the rent. Luckily, punk music lives on.

Will: "I knew it would be my favorite spot. So, what's yours?"
Sa5m: "Now? This is."

Getting the Girl

Will invites Sa5m to come hear I Can't Go On, I'll Go On rehearse. They sound great, but Will isn't really paying attention. He's too busy staring at Sa5m—he'd never really noticed how pretty she is before now! But nothing gets past Charlotte. She notices Will noticing Sa5m, and questions him on the ride home.

Will likes Sa5m as more than a friend, but he's never even kissed a girl before. He has no idea what he's doing. For Will's sake, and strictly educational purposes, Charlotte gives Will a quick kiss. That way he'll know what to do when the time comes with Sa5m.

"I ONLY DO THIS FOR PEOPLE WITH DAZZLING ARTISTIC ABILITY, WHOSE INITIALS ARE W.B."

Charlotte's Tips for Getting the Girl

-Compliment her on something you like about her

-Laugh at her jokes

-Remember things she likes

-Hold her hand

-Be nice to her friends

-And eventually, kiss her!

After Charlotte's practice kiss, Will is ready to ask Sa5m out. On the way home from school, he asks Sa5m to go to the Overlook with him. When they get there, she whips out a book right away, which doesn't make it easy for Will to get her attention. When Will finally does get up the courage to try to kiss her, she won't put the book down! And she's wearing a hat so it's really hard for him to get a shot at her lips. Will acts fast, flicks the hat off, and finally makes his move. And then Sa5m does something totally unexpected—she asks him out!

Sa5m: "Have you ever seen Evil Dead 2?"

Will: "Uh . . . no."

Sa5m: "It's my favorite movie ever. You never get to see it in a theater, but it's playing at the college Saturday night. Would you want to go?"

Will: "Sure. I'd love to."

THE BURNING HOTELS CONCERT

The Burning Hotels are one of the hottest bands in the area and they are going to be competing at BandSlam. Plus, they tied Ben Wheatly and the Glory Dogs for second place at BandSlam last year. So when Charlotte gets the scoop on an underground Burning Hotels concert, she convinces Will that they have to go. It'll be awesome, plus they can get a sneak peek at the competition. Will is extra excited because this is his first concert ever. At the concert, Will can't believe he's there. He has so much fun that he swears he won't wash the stamp off his hand for at least a week.

THE BURNING HOTELS

Charlotte: "Underground club. Saturday night. You're getting a peek at the competition, and I'm not talking Ben Wheatly and the Glory Dogs."

CONCERT DOS AND DON'TS

-Don't wait until the last minute to get your ticket

-Do wear high shoes so you can see over the crowd

-Do hold up your cell phone with the screen lit up and wave it back and forth during slow songs

-Do demand an encore

-Don't scream your head off during slow songs

-Do cheer after every single song

-Don't get caught in the middle of a mosh pit

While Will is having the best night of his life, Sa5m isn't so lucky. She was so excited for her date with Will that she got dressed up and even went to the movie theater without a book! But Will was so distracted by the fact that he was going to a real concert that he completely forgot that their date was on the same night. So Sa5m waits . . . and waits . . . and waits alone at the movie theater. It's her worst nightmare. Being stood up by the one guy she really let herself like is way scarier than Evil Dead 2. Finally she gives up—on the movie and on Will.

EVIL DEAD 2

Perhaps the most amazing horror film ever made. This movie has everything anyone could want in a scary movie. Just be sure not to watch it on a full stomach!

Sa5m and Will's Fight

The next day in class, Will tries joking around with Sa5m, but she is totally ignoring him. He is so confused—he thought things were going so well between them. He tries to catch up with her after class, but she is not in the mood to chat. He's never seen Sa5m so angry.

Will: "Hey. I've called you a billion times. Where have you been?"

Sa5m: "At the movie theater waiting for you."

Will: "Waiting for . . . ? I'm such a jerk. I totally forgot."

Will feels awful about hurting Sa5m. He decides to go to her house and try to apologize again after school. Sa5m's mom is the only one home. After hearing about Will and Sa5m's project, Sa5m's mom decides to show him a video of Sa5m at a talent show when she was younger. Turns out Sa5m can really sing. Will is watching the video of Sa5m singing Bread's "Everything I Own" when she walks in, furious to find him there.

Sa5m: "What are you doing?!"

Will: "Nothing we were just . . . What's wrong? That was amazing."

Sa5m: "She had no business showing that to you."

Will: "Why not? What's the big deal?"

Sa5m: "Why are you here?"

Will: "I came to apologize again."

Sa5m: "Just go."

PRESENTING WILL AND SA5M...

The day has finally come for Sa5m and Will to make their Human Studies presentations. Will is totally nervous. Sa5m won't even talk to him, so he has no clue what she's going to tell the class about him. Sa5m is up first. Everyone is expecting some photos, a movie, or at least a poem, but Sa5m has other plans. She asks the class if anyone knows who Will is. No one does. Then she takes out a mirror and holds it up to everyone's faces so they can see their reflections.

"Will is a reflective surface. He mirrors back at you whatever you want to see. He reflects you back to you. And it's nice for a while. You stop feeling lonely. But then you notice he's doing that with everyone."

She finally gets to Will's seat and holds the mirror up to his face.

"The only one he can't do it for is Will. Because he doesn't have a clue who he is."

Ouch! Based on that, Will is pretty sure Sa5m is still mad at him.

Now it's Will's turn to present. Maybe he still has a chance to win her back. His presentation is a movie he's made called Sa5m You Am. The movie includes all of Sa5m's favorite things except Sa5m isn't actually in the movie. Will took a life-size foam cutout of Sa5m to all her favorite places, "fed" the cutout Sa5m's favorite food, and let the cutout read Sa5m's favorite books. It's the perfect depiction of Sa5m. Clearly, Will cares about her a lot. Smiling, Sa5m looks at Will—how could she possibly stay mad at him now?

THE TRUTH

That afternoon, Will shows up to help out with the after-school program, but there's no sign of Charlotte or the little monsters. A teacher tells Will that the program was cancelled for the day because Charlotte's father passed away. Will tries calling Charlotte, but she doesn't answer.

Will goes straight to Charlotte's house. He sees Ben leaving. Charlotte must have called Ben while she was ignoring Will's phone calls. Never a good sign. When Will approaches Charlotte, she doesn't seem to want to see him. What is going on?

Will: "Charlotte? I'm sorry. I called. I don't know if you got my messages."

Charlotte: "Yeah. I got 'em. Thanks."

Will: "I wish you would have called me."

Will wants Charlotte to know that he and the band are there to support her. He tells her that they'll work around her schedule and do whatever she needs while she deals with her grief. Then Charlotte drops the biggest bomb ever—she's quitting the band! What's even worse is Charlotte confesses that she only ditched her popular cheerleader image because she thought being a nicer person would somehow help her dad get better.

Crushed, Will walks away with tears in his eyes. He's so angry for believing he could actually be friends with someone like Charlotte. What was he thinking? But Will isn't going to let that get him down. He's changed so much in New Jersey and he doesn't want to go back to being the old Will. Not without a fight, anyway.

I Can't Go On, I'll Go On goes on

Will breaks the news to the rest of the band that Charlotte is not coming back. No one is happy about it. But he also convinces them that they don't need Charlotte. They can't quit now after how far they've come. I Can't Go On, I'll Go On must go on!

"I say we refuse to let Charlotte screw this up for us. We've worked too hard. We're doing BandSlam."

The band is still a little skeptical. Charlotte said they could still use the song she wrote, "Someone to Fall Back On," but how can they perform without a lead singer? Will already has a replacement in mind. He remembered that video of Sa5m singing—she can really belt it out. She can be their singer.

Sa5m agrees to join the band, but only as long as everyone focuses! With a new lead singer, Will knows that they can still pull out a win at BandSlam. Everyone is a little tense, but Will does his best to keep the band's spirits up while they get ready for the big day. He even gets T-shirts that say "I Can't Go On" on the front and "I'll Go On" on the back—how cool!

Sa5m: "One week from now we're going to be onstage in front of a thousand people. And you daffodils are not going to embarrass me. Now get your heads in the game and let's melt some faces."

Basher: "Marry me."

Meanwhile, Charlotte hangs out with Ben Wheatly and the Glory Dogs again. Something is wrong though, and she just isn't into it like she used to be. She tries to recapture the magic she's been feeling with I Can't Go On, I'll Go On, but it's just not there. Charlotte has changed. She's not the same girl she used to be.

BANDSLAM

BandSlam is finally here! I Can't Go On, I'll Go On is excited and nervous and totally psyched. Will and Karen can hardly contain themselves as they watch the bands play in the semifinals. Then, the finalists are announced. It's going to be The Daze, the Burning Hotels, Ben Wheatly and the Glory Dogs, and . . .

"FOR THE FIRST TIME EVER, TWO BANDS HAVE MADE THE FINALS FROM THE SAME HIGH SCHOOL. FROM MARTIN VAN BUREN HIGH, IN LODI, NEW JERSEY, I CAN'T GO ON, I'LL GO ON!"

I Can't Go On, I'll Go On is in the finals! Backstage, they watch the Burning Hotels perform. They've never been so nervous. Then, they get even more nervous when Charlotte comes up to them. She's there to apologize. She was so upset by her father dying that she said a lot of things she regrets. She really does care about them and it wasn't just an act. They are her best friends and she's missed them. Can they forgive her? The band isn't convinced, but when Will accepts her apology, the rest of the band does, too. Then Charlotte makes sure they are still going to perform the song she wrote for her dad. It would mean a lot to her.

"You guys rock. And we're singing Phil's song."

"You mean Sa5m's singing Phil's song. Sa5m's the lead singer of this band."

"Of course she is and I'll be the girl in the front screaming my head off while she does."

I CAN'T GO ON, I'LL GO ON'S PERFORMANCE

The make-up session with Charlotte and the band was nice and all, but they still have to perform in the finals! Next up is Ben Wheatly and the Glory Dogs, then it's I Can't Go On, I'll Go On's turn. Ben Wheatly and the Glory Dogs takes the stage and Ben dedicates their song to Charlotte. Everyone in I Can't Go On, I'll Go On goes silent. Ben Wheatly and the Glory Dogs are playing "Someone to Fall Back On"! The same song they are supposed to perform. What is the band going to do? They can't sing the same song! Luckily, Will knows another song that the band knows, and he's sure that Sa5m can rock it out.

"I swear, I didn't know. It's old. Ben knew it. He probably thought he was doing something nice for me. I had no idea, you've got to believe me."

Will buys the band a few minutes, but they don't have long to prepare. Finally, I Can't Go On, I'll Go On takes the stage, tunes up their instruments, and starts playing. They perform Bread's "Everything I Own" and the audience is totally into it. As they finish, the crowd goes wild.

And the Winner Is . . .

Finally, the announcer approaches the mic to reveal the winner.

"And the winner of this year's BandSlam is . . . From Greenwich High School, in Greenwich, Connecticut, The Daze!"

What? As the members of The Daze rush the stage to claim their gigantic trophy, not to mention their gigantic cardboard check, the other bands are crushed. No one saw this coming.

the daze

Will feels worse than he did when he heard that CBGB was closing. All of their hard work was for nothing! But just because they didn't win, doesn't mean that people didn't like them. A video of their performance somehow got onto YouTube and they've got thousands of hits on the band website. I Can't Go On, I'll Go On actually has fans!

"FORGET THE DAZE. THESE GUYS WERE BETTER THAN ANYONE."

GRADUATION

The school year is ending, and for once, Will isn't happy about it. The seniors are graduating, which means that Charlotte, Bug, Omar, Basher, and even Ben won't be around next year. Will is going to miss seeing them every day at school.

After the graduation ceremony, the band decides to go to their favorite spot-Jim's! Even Ben decides to come along.

Ben: "Room for one more? Shotgun!"

Bug: "No way. I called shotgun, like, an hour ago."

Charlotte: "Bug called it. Shotgun must be earned."

Will might be a little bummed that school is over, but he's pretty sure he'll be okay, especially since Sa5m is his girlfriend now. And it's not really the end. I Can't Go On, I'll Go On is going to go on. Will is working on scoring them a record deal and the band is playing gigs around town. Charlotte is even writing them a new song. They have real fans now and they can't let them down.

Nah. It's not the end, it's only the beginning . . .

THE END

Cast of Characters

Aly Michalka as
Charlotte Barnes

Vanessa Hudgens
as Sa5m

Gaelan Connell as
Will Burton

Scott Porter as
Ben Wheatly

Lisa Kudrow as
Karen Burton

Elvy Yost as
Irene Lerman

Charlie Saxton
as Bug

Tim Jo
as Omar

Ryan Donowho
as Basher Martin

Lisa Chung as
Kim Lee

Jonathan Wright
as Dylan

Chris Copeland
as Bo

Kai Roach
as Quinton

NOV 1 9 2009